Through the Heart of the Jungle

For Laura, who roared at the mother asleep in her bed
—J.E

To the two little monkeys I know, Andrew and Ryan Pink
—E.G

tiger tales
an imprint of ME Media, LLC
202 Old Ridgefield Road, Wilton, CT 06897
Published in the United States 2003
Originally published in Great Britain 2003
by Hodder Children's Books
a division of Hodder Headline Limited
Text copyright ©2003 Jonathan Emmett
Illustrations copyright ©2003 Elena Gomez
CIP data is available
First U.S. hardcover edition ISBN 1-58925-029-X
First U.S. paperback edition ISBN 1-58925-380-9
Printed in Hong Kong
1 3 5 7 9 10 8 6 4 2

Through the Heart of the Jungle

by Jonathan Emmett
Illustrated by Elena Gomez

tiger tales

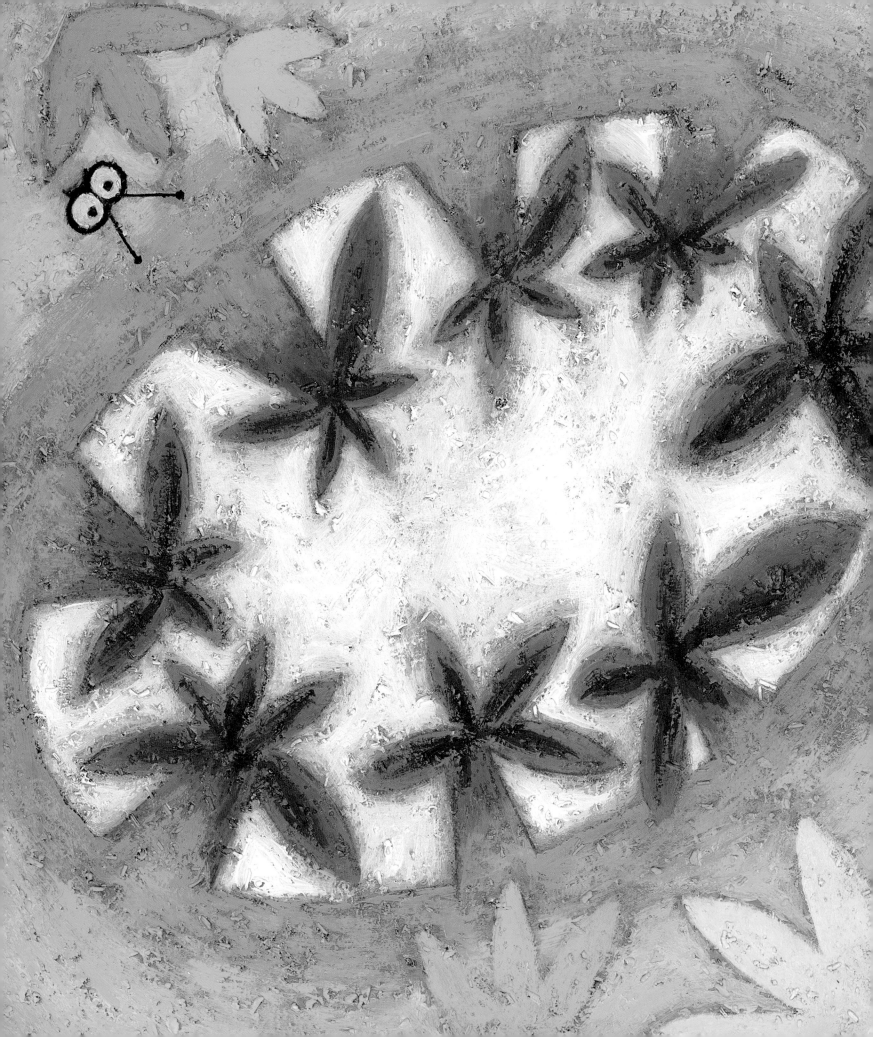

This is the heart of the jungle.

This is the fly,

that buzzed through the heart of the jungle.

that buzzed through the heart of the jungle.

This is the toad with the big googly eye,

that gulped down the spider,
that gobbled the fly,
that buzzed through the heart of the jungle.

that snapped at the toad with the big googly eye,
that gulped down the spider,
that gobbled the fly,
that buzzed through the heart of the jungle.

This is the bear with the long pointy claws,

that jumped on the crocodile
with wide gaping jaws,
that snapped at the toad with the big googly eye,
that gulped down the spider,
that gobbled the fly,
that buzzed through the heart of the jungle.

This is the monkey that let out a shriek,

that startled the bear with the long pointy claws,

that jumped on the crocodile with wide gaping jaws,

that snapped at the toad with the big googly eye,

that gulped down the spider,

that gobbled the fly,

that buzzed through the heart of the jungle.

This is the bird with the bright orange beak,

that flew at the monkey that let out a shriek,

that startled the bear with the long pointy claws,

that jumped on the crocodile with wide gaping jaws,

that snapped at the toad with the big googly eye,

that gulped down the spider,

that gobbled the fly,

that buzzed through the heart of the jungle.

This is the snake that slithered and slunk,

that hissed at the bird with the bright orange beak,
that flew at the monkey that let out a shriek,
that startled the bear with the long pointy claws,
that jumped on the crocodile with wide gaping jaws,
that snapped at the toad with the big googly eye,
that gulped down the spider,
that gobbled the fly,

that buzzed through the heart of the jungle.

This is the elephant, swinging its trunk,

that swatted the snake that slithered and slunk,

that hissed at the bird with the bright orange beak,

that flew at the monkey that let out a shriek,

that startled the bear with the long pointy claws,

that jumped on the crocodile with wide gaping jaws,

that snapped at the toad with the big googly eye,

that gulped down the spider,

that gobbled the fly,

that buzzed through the heart of the jungle.

And what
started
the trouble?

Well last,
but not least . . .

that roared at
    the elephant,
        swinging its trunk,

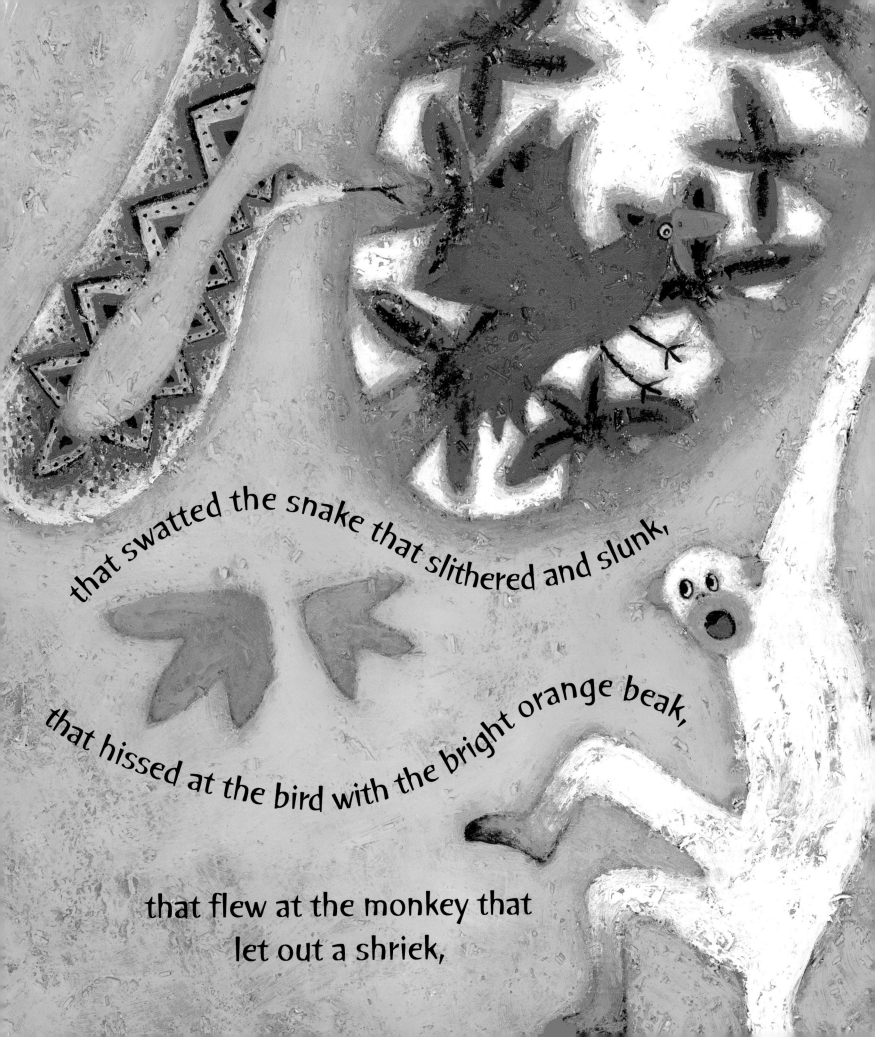

that swatted the snake that slithered and slunk,

that hissed at the bird with the bright orange beak,

that flew at the monkey that
let out a shriek,

that startled
the bear
with the
long
pointy
claws,

that jumped on the crocodile with wide gaping jaws,

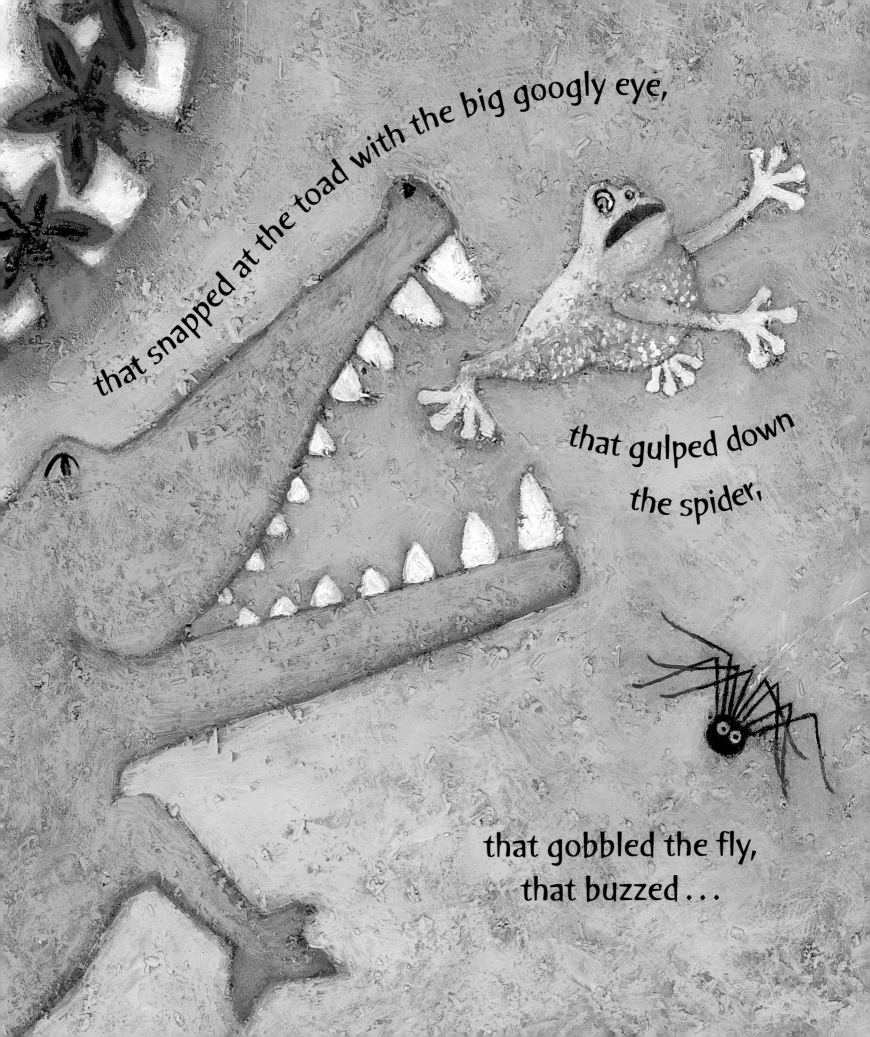

that snapped at the toad with the big googly eye,

that gulped down
the spider,

that gobbled the fly,
that buzzed . . .

through the heart of the jungle!